CAPTAIN SMALL PIG

Martin Waddell   Susan Varley

ANDERSEN PRESS

One day Old Goat and Turkey took Small Pig down to Blue Lake.
They found a little red boat.
"I want to go for a row!" Small Pig said, dancing about.
"Turkeys don't go in boats," Turkey said.
"Neither do goats," said Old Goat, but he climbed into the boat,
and they rowed off on Blue Lake.

"I want to fish for whales!" said Small Pig.

"There aren't any whales in Blue Lake," said Turkey.

"There might be a very small whale," said Old Goat, and he tied a string to an oar, so Small Pig could try his whale fishing.

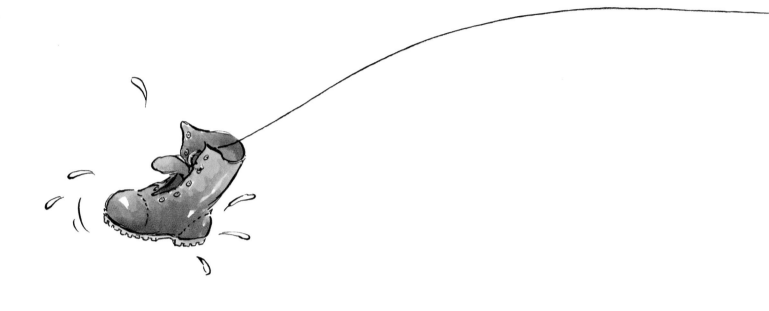

Small Pig didn't catch any whales,
but he caught an old boot,
which was almost as good . . .
you can store lots of things in a boot.

"I want to row now!" said Small Pig.

"You're too small to row!" Turkey objected.

"Of course you can row!" said Old Goat.

Small Pig could only manage one oar at time so he rowed . . .

round and round . . .

. . . round and round . . . round and round . . .

but he rowed the boat all by himself.

"I'm Captain Commander!" Small Pig said.
Turkey just nodded his head, sleepily.
"Aye aye, Captain Small Pig!" said Old Goat.
"You are in charge of this boat!"

"But I'm too tired to row any more!" Small Pig said.

"I knew you would be!" said Turkey.

"Just let the boat drift," yawned Old Goat sleepily.

"But keep your hand on the tiller!"

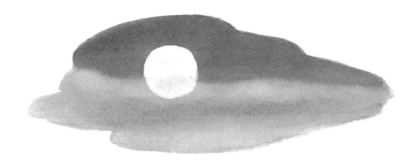

As the moon rose, the boat drifted back through the reeds, toward the shore.

Small Pig was . . . sort of . . . steering the boat. And then . . . Small Pig . . . sort of . . . wasn't steering the boat. He'd fallen asleep holding his boot.

The boat was . . . sort of . . . steering itself.

"My turn to steer!" sighed old Goat. He shifted the sleeping Small Pig, and took over the tiller.

As they drew towards the jetty the boat rocked . . .

one way . . . .

and then the other . . . until . . . .

SPLOOOOOSH!

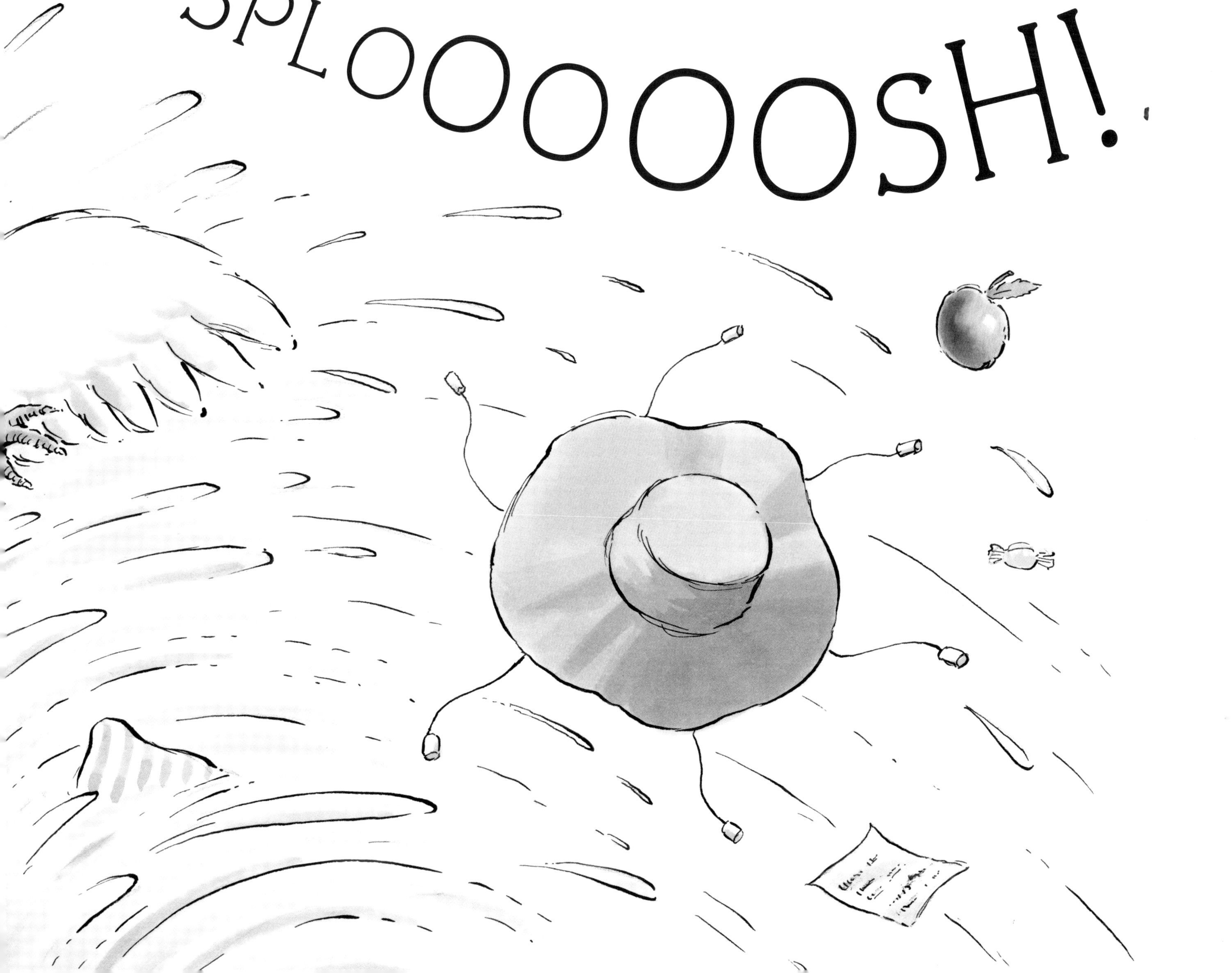

"GRRR . . .

OH-AH . . .

GLUG-UG!" spluttered Turkey.

"*Shhhhh!* We mustn't wake up Captain Small Pig!" Old Goat warned Turkey.

They carried Small Pig all the way home, wrapped warm in a rug, and they tucked him up cosy in bed.

Small Pig slept . . . and he dreamt . . . of a lovely day out
in a boat with good friends on Blue Lake . . .

. . . the day he was Captain Small Pig.